NINE LIVES
NEWTON

FOR MUTTI AND BEN

'A CAT HAS NINE LIVES.
FOR THREE HE PLAYS,
FOR THREE HE STRAYS
AND FOR THE LAST THREE HE STAYS.'

ANCIENT PROVERB

SIMON & SCHUSTER
First published in Great Britain in 2020 by Simon & Schuster UK Ltd
1st Floor, 222 Gray's Inn Road, London, WC1X 8HB
A CBS Company

Text and illustrations copyright © 2020 Alice McKinley

ISBN: 978-1-4711-8118-4 (PB) • ISBN: 978-1-4711-8119-1 (eBook)
Printed in China • 10 9 8 7 6 5 4 3 2 1

NINE LIVES NEWTON

ALICE McKINLEY

SIMON & SCHUSTER
London   New York   Sydney   Toronto   New Delhi

HELLO!

MY NAME IS NEWTON

AND I'VE JUST FOUND OUT THAT I HAVE

NINE LIVES!

NOT JUST ONE, OR TWO, OR THREE, BUT NINE!

AND IF I'VE GOT NINE LIVES, THAT MEANS I CAN DO
ALL MY FAVOURITE THINGS . . .

BUT NOW I CAN BE MUCH MORE DARING!

I'M OFF TO LIVE MY LIFE
DANGEROUSLY.

OH DEAR.

NEWTON! WAIT!
YOU'VE MADE A MISTAKE!

IF I'M LIVING LIFE DANGEROUSLY,
THAT MEANS I CAN DIG THE DEEPEST HOLES . . .

NEWTON!

SCORPIONS
- OH-SO-DANGEROUS
- POISONOUS STING
- SHARP PINCERS
- ANGRY FACE

I CAN POO
ANYWHERE I LIKE . . .

I CAN PRACTISE MY BEST BARK . . .

. . . AND I CAN RUN,

AND RUN,

AND RUN!

BUT SOMETIMES YOU HAVE TO FIND
SOMEWHERE NICE AND QUIET TO RELAX.

THIS IS JUST PERFECT . . .

NEWTON! STOP!
YOU HAVEN'T GOT
NINE LIVES!

oH!

PHEW, THAT WAS CLOSE!
YOU KNOW, IT'S A GOOD THING
YOU TOLD ME . . .

OR ELSE SOMEONE COULD'VE
REALLY GOT HURT.

WELL, I MAY NOT HAVE NINE LIVES, BUT . . .

OH NO. HERE WE GO AGAIN.

NEWTON!

WAITTTTTTT!!!